Beyond the

Tony Parsons is the author of *Man and Boy,* which won the Book of the Year prize. His other novels – *One For My Baby, Man and Wife, The Family Way, Stories We Could Tell, My Favourite Wife, Starting Over* and *Men from the Boys* – were all bestsellers. He was recently writer-in-residence at Heathrow. *Departures*, his first collection of stories, is the result. Tony is the son and grandson of sailors and lives in London.

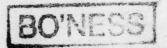

Beyond the Bounty

Tony Parsons

HARPER

Harper
An imprint of HarperCollins*Publishers*
77–85 Fulham Palace Road,
Hammersmith, London W6 8JB

www.harpercollins.co.uk

First published in Great Britain by
HarperCollins*Publishers* 2012

Copyright © Tony Parsons 2012

Tony Parsons asserts the moral right to
be identified as the author of this work

A catalogue record for this book is
available from the British Library

ISBN: 978-0-00-744913-2

Set in ITC Stone Serif by Palimpsest Book Production Limited,
Falkirk, Stirlingshire

Printed and bound in Great Britain by

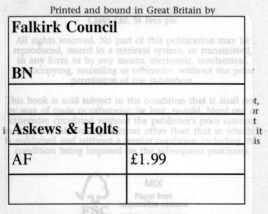

www.fsc.org   FSC C007454

FSC™ is a non-profit international organisation established to promote
the responsible management of the world's forests. Products carrying the
FSC label are independently certified to assure consumers that they come
from forests that are managed to meet the social, economic and
ecological needs of present and future generations,
and other controlled sources.

Find out more about HarperCollins and the environment at
www.harpercollins.co.uk/green

For my father, the old sailor who told me,
'One hand for the ship – one hand
for yourself.'

Author's Note

The mutiny on HMS *Bounty* occurred in the South Seas on 28th April 1789.

Eighteen sailors led by Fletcher Christian rose up against the ship's cruel commanding officer, Captain William Bligh.

The men who joined the mutiny set Captain Bligh and those loyal to him adrift in a small boat, many thousands of miles from the known world.

After sailing further, the mutineers settled on the island of Pitcairn, which was not yet on any map. Here the *Bounty* was burned to stop it being found by the Royal Navy.

Nearly twenty years later the American trading ship *Topaz* discovered the secret community on Pitcairn. They found nine women, many children and just one man left alive.

This is his story.

Contents

1. A Mighty Fire   1

2. The Angry Widow   12

3. Wives of the *Bounty*   21

4. The Last of the Rum   32

5. The Woman on the Cliff   41

6. Crime and Punishment   52

7. The Shipwrecked Sailor   59

8. The Best Time   67

9. Civil War   71

10. King of the World   78

1

A Mighty Fire

Our ship, the *Bounty*, was made of English oak and it made a mighty fire.

We watched her burn from the shore of the tiny island. She was the ship that had been our home, our prison and our mad dream of freedom. The ship that had carried us to the end of the world.

It burned.

And before this night was over, our captain would burn with it.

The night was full of the sound of the animals we had brought ashore and the crackle of burning wood. But there were no human sounds. Not until our captain howled with pain.

'You burn our ship?' cried Fletcher Christian. 'You fools! Then how will we ever go home?'

We watched him row out to the *Bounty*. We made no move to help or to hinder him. We just stood watching on the narrow beach of soft sand at the bottom of steep white cliffs.

What a strange little party we were – eight

English sailors from the *Bounty*, six men and eleven women from Tahiti, one of them with a babe in arms. After our many adventures on the rocky road to Eden, and after leaving some of our fellow sailors on Tahiti, that was all that we had left to build a new world. One of the women was crying. This was Maimiti, daughter of the King of Tahiti, a great beauty and wife of our captain, Fletcher Christian.

We saw him reach the *Bounty*, climb on deck and go below. He stood out like a little black insect against the flames. We watched him throw useless buckets of water on the burning masts, the flaming sails and the smoking deck.

We knew it was a battle that he could never win. When his clothes began to smoke and flame, we knew he knew it too.

We watched him come back. Slowly, wearily. Rowing with the good arm he had left.

There was not much to be done. He was badly burned and the life was already ebbing out of him. We lay him down on that narrow sandy beach. We gave him water. The women comforted his wife.

And I held him as he died.

Some of the men wept.

The Tahitians who thought he was some kind of god. And even a few of the English seamen, who also placed him high above other men.

I held him, but I was dry-eyed. Because I had never liked Fletcher Christian.

Mister Fletcher Christian.

That's always what he was to me – *Mister* Fletcher bloody Christian.

From the first moment I saw him, looking dapper in his fine midshipman's clothes on the deck of HMS *Bounty* as we set sail on 23rd December 1787 from Spithead, to the last moment I saw him dying of those terrible burns more than two years later on the beach of Pitcairn.

I never cared for the fellow.

Oh, I know the ladies in smart drawing rooms back in London probably still get all weepy when they think of Mister Fletcher Christian – so tall, so handsome, so doomed. And I knew men who would have followed Fletcher Christian to the gates of hell and beyond.

But he was not for me.

I knew him. Not the legend but the man. I saw his kindness and his courage when he faced down our first captain, William Bligh.

I knew Fletcher Christian and I choked on the smell of his burning flesh as he died in my embrace. And I could see clear enough what the rest of the world saw in him too.

He was blue-eyed and fair-haired, broad-shouldered and topping six foot. Clean of mind – at least until he fixed his telescope on those

3

Tahitian maids – and clean of limb. Brave as a young lion.

He stood up to Bligh's foul cruelty when it would have been the easy thing to go below deck and puff his pipe and read his Bible. Instead Fletcher Christian led us, and he steered the *Bounty* and the mutineers into history.

Even at the moment of his death, Fletcher's heart was made of the same sturdy English oak as our ship. But I believe that we broke his heart when we torched the *Bounty* as she lay in the bay.

We burned her to avoid detection. We burned her to prevent desertion.

And most of all we burned her to avoid Fletcher Christian having the bright idea of going home to dear old England to explain our actions to some judge who would hang us all.

For that was what he wanted – our leader, our young lion, our Mister Fletcher Christian – he wanted to explain our mutiny to those in England.

The rest of us were willing to settle for watching fifty years of sunsets with some Tahitian maid under a palm tree. And keeping the hangman's rope from our mutinous necks.

But he was good, you see.

Mister Fletcher Christian. A good man. An honest man. They all loved that goodness in Fletcher Christian, even as he burned to a crisp under the tropical moon.

The men. The women. The world. But what they loved about Mister Fletcher Christian was what made me, in some secret chamber of my heart, turn away from the man.

For it was the very *goodness* of Mister Fletcher Christian that stuck in my throat. He carried his goodness around like a bloody halo, expecting the rest of the world to give it a polish every now and then. He carried his goodness like Christ with his cross on the road to Calvary.

And our captain was crucified upon that cross.

Mr Christian – was ever a legend more fittingly named? – thought he was better than other men.

More moral. More noble. More good.

Perhaps he was right. Perhaps.

He certainly always thought it. He had the rock-solid confidence of the upper-class Englishman.

A bit of a snob, our Mister Christian.

He may have believed that our first cruel captain, Bligh, was wicked and evil and a monster. It is true that Bligh would smile at the sight of the whip being brought out as if it was the sun breaking through grey clouds, or an orange in a stocking on Christmas Day.

But I reckon that Fletcher Christian also believed that William Bligh was from the gutter.

I reckon that Mr Christian thought that rough William Bligh was little better than the scum and rascals who made up the crew of the *Bounty* on our mad mission to bring back breadfruit from the South Seas of the Pacific Ocean.

Fletcher Christian looked down on William Bligh. And he would have looked down on Bligh even if he had spoon-fed us rum from dawn to dusk.

Still, Fletcher Christian was impressive. I will give him that.

They are building their bloody Empire on the likes of Fletcher Christian. They think that men like him (the brightest, the best) are leading the likes of me (the rankest, the worst).

Fletcher sipped his port. The men got roaring drunk on rot-gut rum. Fletcher fluttered his eyelashes at the ladies. We whored. Fletcher was a cultivated man. We could just about make our mark if you were to guide our hand. You get the picture.

Fletcher Christian was a gentleman.

More than us. And more than Bligh. But *better* than the rest of us? Mister Fletcher Christian clearly thought so.

But in my experience of this wicked world, all men are much the same.

The *Bounty* burned all night.

As the sun came up over the South Seas, the ship that had carried us so far was meeting its end in flames fifty feet high.

It was a day as close to Paradise as I ever saw in this world. The sky above the island was so blue that it made your heart ache to behold such beauty.

A soft breeze was moving through the palm trees like a mother's sigh. And the heat – it was that soothing heat that we found on the island, that calming heat we found at the end of the world.

Even as I held my dying captain in his final minutes, I was not sorry that we had burned the *Bounty*. Because we wanted this Eden to last.

We did not want to go back to England. There, we would have to tell our story and to make our case. To throw ourselves at the dubious mercy of some bewigged bastard of a judge.

After much careful reflection, we had no wish to sail back to England and face justice that would have had us all dangling on the end of a rope. We would hang – twitching and shitting and eyes bulging, our tongues turning black as our dear old mothers wept and the crowd roared with delighted laughter.

Go back to that?

No thank you, Mister Christian, sir.

But his goodness was calling him back to England. And then his goodness called him to that burning ship. And finally his goodness was calling him to Heaven.

'Ned, I am done for,' he croaked. 'Tonight I shall walk the streets of glory, and sit with angels in the realm of the Lord.'

You could see he was quite looking forward to it. The angels. The clouds. The business of comparing halos. The way he told it, dying was like shore leave that lasted for all eternity. Without the pox and the sore heads. You could see the attraction.

Then he writhed and twisted with that terrible pain. Fire is a terrible way to go. Give me water. Give me my lungs full of salt water in Davey Jones' locker for a year rather one minute of the pain that Mister Fletcher Christian endured at the end of his short and famous life.

The men were crying. The women too. The men were crying like women and the women were crying like banshees. What a racket! I had to bark at them to shut their traps. For I could hardly hear the words of the dying man in my arms.

'Ned,' he said. 'Oh, Ned Young. Why did you do it? Oh, how could you burn our proud *Bounty*?'

'Because we can't go home, sir,' I blubbered. Now the rest of them had started me off and I was sobbing like a milkmaid who has had her best bucket hidden by a stable lad. 'Because we can't go home where nothing is waiting but the rope.'

'No, Ned – it is still our old and beloved

England,' he gasped. 'Justice, Ned. The truth.' He fought for breath here, for he was overcome by the pain. 'What is right and what is wrong,' he continued. 'Standing for liberty against tyranny. Standing for Christian values in the face of all that is cruel and wicked. That was our choice – the way of Captain Bligh or my way, Ned.'

As though all goodness and right belonged to him alone. He coughed a bit at this point. Mostly blood, although also some yellow substance which did not look too promising.

'They would have listened,' says he.

'They would have listened, all right,' says I. 'They would have had a good old listen and then they would have made us dangle.'

But even a cold, hard-hearted scoundrel such as myself could not fail to be moved by the death of Mister Fletcher Christian.

My eyes ran with tears and I knew that, despite everything, I loved him.

Not that I ever liked him much.

But I can't deny that I loved him.

I could feel the fire in my blood. The *Bounty* crackled and shrieked like a living thing. It died hissing and spitting as it dropped its masts into the boiling water. And then, just as the sky was turning pale pink in the east, the *Bounty* collapsed beneath the sea.

For a few minutes there were wispy trails of

grey smoke curling from the surface, and then they were gone too.

It was as if our ship had never existed.

'Ned,' Fletcher Christian whispered. And it was no more than a faint whisper now, this close to the end. 'Don't leave me. Don't let me go alone, Ned.'

'I'm here,' I sobbed, holding him as tight as I could without causing him even more pain. 'I'm here, and here I will stay. I shall not go until you are gone. I promise you that. You have my word, Mister Fletcher Christian, sir.'

'Oh, Ned,' he said. 'The pain.'

I placed my hand over his nose and mouth. 'There, there,' I said. 'There, there – rest your eyes, Mister Christian, sir. Rest those blue eyes of yours for just a moment, sir.'

His eyes widened as I leaned into him, pushing down harder over his nose and mouth, making quite sure that he would not be breathing much more of that sweet tropical air.

The eyes of Mister Fletcher Christian slowly began to close.

I have big hands, you see.

Big hands made hard by twenty-five years before the mast.

Stopping a dying man from breathing is about as hard for me as it is for your grandmother to fill her pipe.

'You're right, sir,' I said. 'The angels are waiting for you. They have been waiting all along. You have been right all along, Mister Fletcher Christian, sir. Right about everything.'

Heaven was calling him.

Loud and clear.

Even above the weeping and wailing of the men and the women, and even above the terrible sound of the *Bounty* dying in the bay, you could hear Heaven calling Mister Fletcher Christian to his reward.

And I confess on these pages that these large and hardened hands of mine helped that good young gentleman on his way.

It felt like the least I could do.

2

The Angry Widow

I climbed to the top of the cliffs and I looked back on our island.

It was like looking at Paradise. Our island, Pitcairn, was Paradise.

Pitcairn is a tiny garden in the middle of an endless ocean. A densely wooded rock in the middle of nowhere. Just two miles square. And the loneliest island in the South Seas.

We had looked for it long and hard before we found it.

The *Bounty* had visited more than thirty islands before we landed on Pitcairn. Yes, more than thirty islands bobbing in the South Seas, and they all had something wrong with them.

There were islands where the natives thought they might decorate their grass huts by putting our heads on the ends of muddy sticks.

There were islands with so little water we would have died of thirst before the year was out.

There were islands with nothing to eat. Islands with nothing to drink. Islands where the natives came screaming out of the bushes and chased us back to our long boat. We saw them all.

And then we saw Pitcairn, our beautiful island in the sun. The last home that any of us would ever know.

It was a place of rough beauty. The steep cliffs. The jagged rocks in the bay and the wild sea beyond. The craggy green hills. The deep blue of the sea and the lighter blue of the sky.

There was fresh water and food galore. It was uninhabited. And the sea winds made it far cooler than Tahiti.

Pitcairn was perfect.

We almost missed it. We almost sailed right by. Not because it is such a tiny speck in that endless expanse of blue water that men call the Pacific Ocean.

No, we almost sailed straight past our future home because, according to every single map in the King's navy, Pitcairn was not there.

The maps were wrong.

Pitcairn was charted wrong on the *Bounty*'s map, which means that it was charted wrong on all of them. Mister Christian spotted it. According to the map, Pitcairn was meant to be 150 miles from where God had seen fit to drop it.

It was too good to be true. The men could scarcely believe their luck. Pitcairn was a paradise that showed itself on no man's map.

Even old Fletcher had a smile on his dark and handsome chops for once.

We would hide ourselves forever on the only island in the Pacific that, as far as the King's navy was concerned, did not exist.

It felt as if we had stumbled into the Garden of Eden. The soil was rich and fertile, and there was food galore. Game. Yam. Papaya. Pineapples. Watermelons. Mandarins. Grapefruit. Lemon. Limes. And breadfruit – bloody breadfruit!

We all had a good laugh at the sight of breadfruit.

For breadfruit was the reason for the *Bounty*'s doomed mission to the ends of the earth. We were meant to bring back a cargo of breadfruit so that it could be fed to the slaves of the West Indies. And if it kept those busy fellows going until teatime then the British powers that be were going to feed breadfruit to the entire Empire.

Captain William Bligh was to be to breadfruit what Sir Walter Raleigh had been to the potato. That was the grand plan. Except the *Bounty* never made it home.

And the only breadfruit that I ever picked went straight into my belly. Or the sea, when we were throwing them at Bligh's head as we cast him adrift in his little boat to drown in shark-rotten waters, or get his private parts sliced off by unfriendly natives, or – my guess as to Bligh's fate – starve to death.

But our diet was now better than anything the King had ever dished up when we served in his navy.

There was game on Pitcairn – mostly birds, with lovely crunchy bones – and those wild blue waters teemed with fish. Lobster, yellowtail, Wahoo, snapper, cod. And fish that none of us had never seen before and did not know the names of. These we had to name ourselves – as though we were the Lord himself, naming His creatures.

A soft southern breeze made the climate more like a hot English summer than the furnace we had known in Tahiti or on board the *Bounty*. Work was easier on Pitcairn, and soon some of us were growing carrots, peas, beans, yams, sweet potatoes and sugarcane (while some of us got drunk on what was left of the rum).

Most importantly, they – the Royal Navy – would never find us here. And even if they did – which they wouldn't! – find Pitcairn by accident, as we had found it, then we would see them coming.

The only access to the island was the bay where we moored our ship. Bounty Bay, we came to call it – the first place on the island to be given a name.

I looked out at Bounty Bay now from the top

of those white cliffs. While a gentle breeze moved my hair, and all of Paradise lay spread below me, I remembered the *Bounty* as she burned.

The fire had been brighter than the stars, and brighter than the moon. If there had been a ship within one hundred miles, then they would have seen that fire and we would have dangled on a rope in Jamaica or Java or wherever they decided to give us a fair trial before they strung us up.

But nobody saw the fire.

In that great blue expanse of ocean, we were all alone now.

It was like being the last men and women alive in the world.

I stretched my arms to the heavens and let out a breath that I felt I might have been holding for a lifetime.

Then I walked back down the green hill and we buried Fletcher Christian.

'Perhaps we should help them, Ned,' said John Adams to me, stooping to whisper in my ear so that none of the others should hear.

We were watching a few of the men from Tahiti dig Fletcher Christian's final resting place. Our dead leader's body was wrapped in an oily sail-cloth and his young widow was weeping and wailing over it.

I looked up at John. I was a big man but he was

bigger. In his meaty hands he held the ship's Bible.

'Help them?' I said, not getting his drift. I turned back to the fresh grave and barked a command. 'Put your back into it, you idle savages, or you will feel the end of my boot!' I cried, offering them support in their labours. 'Soon the sun will be high and the body will be getting ripe!'

The copper-skinned Tahitians looked up at me and grinned with apologies. Then they mopped their brows and carried on digging.

'If we are to live in this place,' said John to me, 'then surely all men must be equal.'

I nodded sagely. 'Of course, John,' I said. Then I paused. 'But that doesn't include the Tahitians too, does it?'

'Indeed it does, Ned,' John said. 'Tahitians and Englishmen alike. This is our home now. If it is to be a more just and Christian world than the hell William Bligh made for us aboard the *Bounty*, then surely all men must have the same rights – whatever their tribe.' John got a look full of zeal in his eyes. I glanced down at the battered old Bible in his hands. 'And that means we find food together, and we build shelter together, and we dig graves together!'

I murmured vaguely. Then I nodded towards the grave. Only the raven-haired tops of those Tahitian heads were visible now. 'Well,' I said, 'I think they've almost finished.'

The Tahitians clambered out and we all formed a circle around the grave. And what a strange little tribe we were, those of us starting from scratch on this uncharted island.

Eight English seamen, some of us still wearing the tattered rags we had worn on the *Bounty*, others in the light cotton wraps worn by the natives – kirtles, they were called.

Six Tahitian men who had helped us crew the *Bounty* after we left half of our fellow mutineers on Tahiti.

Eleven women of all shapes and sizes, plus a baby boy who had been born on the quarterdeck of the *Bounty*.

One of the women gently led Fletcher's widow to the graveside so we could get on with the funeral. 'Maimiti,' said the woman who comforted her, 'Maimiti.' It always sounded like 'My Meaty' to my scurvy English ears.

Maimiti was across the black hole from me and I had a good look at her. She was the kind of woman that a man can't stop looking at.

I realised that I had always enjoyed looking at her. Though when our master and commander was husband to her, it had to be done out of the corner of my eye, on the sly.

We were silent apart from the choking sobs of Maimiti. The English mutineers. The Tahitians. Even the baby was sleeping.

John Adams opened his Bible and said a few words.

'Today we say goodbye to our fallen leader and our beloved brother,' said John, his voice booming across the open grave. 'Master's mate and true captain of His Majesty's Ship *Bounty* – Fletcher Christian.'

John gave the nod and a couple of our crew began lowering his body into the grave. The Tahitian man next to me – no more than a boy, really – was examining the dirt under his fingernails. I gave him a quick kick and then he gave the funeral service his full attention.

'Fletcher believed that we would find no happiness here,' said John. 'That we would be forever hiding and shivering like convicts. That life here would be another way of dying. As we say goodbye to our fallen brother, and as we dedicate our lives here to living in the light of the Lord, we hope to prove him wrong . . .'

It was impressive stuff from John Adams – full of fire and brimstone, the wrath of God and the promise of streets of gold. But I was not really listening. I was too busy watching Maimiti on the other side of the grave, noticing how her body curved under that thin native dress.

She was the loveliest of the lot. The fairest woman I have ever seen. Her eyes flashed with black light. Her skin looked as though it had never spent one day out of the sun. Her teeth were white as bone.

The King's daughter, so they said. I believe he had several hundred of them.

But this one here, she was said to be the favourite child of King Tynah of Tahiti. And a real king he was too. Although a king in these parts was not quite the same as a king back home. I believe His Majesty King Tynah was the type of monarch who had fifty wives and wiped his royal arse with his hand.

But still, she was the daughter of the king of Tahiti. Maimiti, Maimiti. Daughter of the king, widow of the captain, the most beautiful sight in all of our tropical Eden.

John didn't look up from his old Bible.

Ashes to ashes, dust to dust. All of that. The usual mournful farewells.

But the other men – Tahitians and English, boys and men – kept glancing up from Fletcher Christian's grave to steal a look at his young widow.

There she stood, all curvy and weeping and alone. I could see it in their eyes and I felt it too.

Maimiti wasn't like the rest. You couldn't buy her with a bucket of glass beads and a bite of your banana.

She had to be won.

3

Wives of the *Bounty*

The women.

It was all about the women.

They told our tale as if it were the story of men. But they got it wrong by making it a story about the men.

The men of the King's ship *Bounty*. The men who served under Captains Bligh and Christian. The men who rose up when the cruelty and the sadism and the lash became too much to bear.

A story about men.

Somewhere in my bones I knew they would tell our tale all round the world for generations. In the alehouses of Portsmouth and London and Liverpool. In the whorehouses of Shanghai and Alexandria and Lagos. In the ten thousand docks where the King's navy lay anchor.

And in another kind of dock in Jamaica. The kind of dock where you stand in chains and you can hear the *tock-tock-tock* sound of them building your gallows out in the yard.

Men at sea. Men with the cat-o'-nine-tails

taking the skin off their backs. Men who could take no more. That was us. And it was all true.

But the story of the *Bounty* was really about the women.

It is true that Bligh was a cruel and cold-hearted captain who believed the men who served under him were the scum of England (he was probably right). But I had seen and served with other English naval captains who were just as cruel, and just as quick to reach for the whip.

That was our navy. Those were our lives. Here was our glorious Empire.

But the mutiny that seized the *Bounty* would never have happened if it wasn't for the women we found on Tahiti.

Those angels of the South Seas. So soft, so brown, so gentle. So totally unlike anything we had ever known in our hard, sea-faring lives.

Yes, Bligh was a wicked devil, but we had seen his like before. And if we had kept taking the King's shilling, we would have seen his like again. But when would we ever again find women like the women we found in Tahiti?

They looked into our broken, toothless faces and they saw something that nobody in our lives had ever seen. Not even our mothers. The women of Tahiti looked into our scarred, battered features and seemed to see fine gentlemen rather than a bunch of stinking sea dogs.

Certainly they were fooling themselves.

Certainly our Tahitian wives gave us more credit than we had ever been given by a working girl in a Southampton knocking shop.

Or perhaps an English sailor is as exotic and strange to a brown Tahitian maid as she is to him. I don't know.

After being at sea for ten months, we stayed in Tahiti for five months. Five months while we collected 1,015 breadfruit plants (somebody counted them, although it wasn't me).

You see, although I can't explain the gardening of the matter to you, we all understood that the breadfruits had to reach a certain stage of their growing before we could transport them to the slaves in the West Indies.

'Men,' said Bligh one day, frowning like Moses down from the mountain. 'Listen now. The breadfruit is vital to the economic life of the British Empire. We must drop our anchor for a good while in Tahiti.'

That was fine by our lights. It gave us plenty of time to get to know Tahiti. And the women. We explored every lush tropical inch of the island, and of the women.

We were more than sailors on shore leave. It was not just a matter of spreading our wanton seed. Spend five months in Tahiti and man will find one woman he could spend the rest of his days with. Or perhaps more than one.

In Tahiti, we knew loving like we had never known. And we knew love.

After knowing such sweetness, how could we live on without it? After glimpsing Paradise – no, after setting anchor in Paradise for five months of bliss and free bananas – how could we sail away to the lonely, loveless sea?

That was what made our voyage away from Tahiti unbearable. Not William Bligh, whose evil ways were standard issue in the King's navy, inhumanity being the British Empire's most loyal and faithful servant.

During our stay in Tahiti, Bligh ordered our hides to be flogged almost on a daily basis, usually because some light-fingered natives had made off with goods that belonged to His Majesty King George. Yet the flogging didn't seem quite so bad when you could spend the night making love under the palm trees with the South Sea moonlight shining its silvery light on your hairy English arse.

We put up with Bligh's cruel ways so long as we had our women. But after we sailed with our cargo of breadfruit, leaving our women weeping in their little canoes and cutting their heads with rocks, as is the South Sea custom at times of grief, that is when we said, 'Damn your blood, William Bligh! And damn your eyes!'

It wasn't because of the constant flogging that we wanted to string up our captain. It was because he robbed us of our women.

The *Bounty* was taken by Fletcher Christian because he pined for his Maimiti just as the rest of us pined for the dusky maidens that we had left back on that Tahitian shore.

We knew we were for the noose if they ever caught us. We knew we would never see England and home and family again unless we saw it briefly with a rope around our necks.

We knew that we would be exiles forever for taking the *Bounty*.

But we did it for the women.

And the men who stuck with Bligh (and who probably followed him to the bottom of the sea, I shouldn't wonder, or starved to death, or gave their bollocks for a native to wear as earrings), they left because of the women.

The other women.

The women back home.

The wives who were nursing newborn babies or raising small children. Or the older wives who they had loved for a lifetime. Or the sweethearts who were yet to become wives. All of it was about the women. Those who mutinied. Those who got into Bligh's leaky boat.

The Bligh loyalists – that was what we called them, our former shipmates who wanted no part of the mutiny – got into that little boat and paddled away for their women just as surely as we sailed back to Tahiti for the women that we had left behind.

Even Bligh had a wife. I suppose he must have loved her, as much as Bligh was capable of loving anything. Certainly he was as celibate as a novice monk during our time in Tahiti. Bligh never touched a Tahitian lass with so much as a dirty breadfruit.

The women ruled our world.

Our story wasn't about breadfruit. And it wasn't about Bligh's cruelty. And it wasn't even about treating men like vermin.

It was about the women.

And even now – with Bligh no doubt dead, and with the *Bounty* burned, and Fletcher Christian freshly buried, and with us willingly shipwrecked for evermore . . . Even now as our mad adventure reached its bloody conclusion on the secret island of Pitcairn, I thought to myself that it was still all about the women.

I watched the slim yet curvy figure of Maimiti walk away from the grave of Fletcher Christian, the man she had loved. Her black hair tumbled down over her lovely face.

The king's daughter. The captain's widow. I admired the way her rump rolled rhythmically up and down as she walked.

'Someone should comfort that poor child,' I said to John Adams, who was sitting on the grass hunched over his open Bible, muttering to himself about the wrath of the Lord.

He looked up from the good book.

'That's very thoughtful of you, Ned,' he said. 'Shall I ask one of the women to stay with her?'

'No, I'll do it,' I said, perhaps a little too quickly. But my Bible-thumping shipmate got a teary glint in his eye.

'You're a good man, Ned Young,' he said, and I scarpered off after Maimiti before he had a chance to change his mind.

She was off up a grassy path that led away from our settlement. As I trotted after her, I encountered some drunken piece of scum lounging against a palm tree with a bottle of rum in his hand. It was John Mills, a gunner's mate, and as different to Bible-loving John Adams as chalk is to cheese.

He leered at me in his insolent fashion. (As a general rule they are a rough lot, the gunner's mates.)

'Off to sample some of the captain's port, are we, Ned?' he said, rolling his eyes and grinning foolishly and almost puking his guts up with merriment.

'Still your tongue, John Mills,' I said.

I leaned down and gave him the back of my hand across his stupid face and he didn't like the taste of it as much as his rum. But he was too drunk to stand up and fight me like a man.

I moved quickly on, having for a moment lost sight of the lovely Maimiti's magnificent backside (surely one of the finest views in all the South Seas).

The drunken gunner's mate called after me.

'You can't do that to me, Ned Young! There are no more officers and men! Now there are only men, Ned! You cannot strike me!'

I answered him over my shoulder.

'Examine your broken nose,' I shouted, 'and you will find that I can strike you well enough.'

Then I had a bit of a chuckle to myself until I saw Maimiti on her knees in the shadow of the palms, crying her pretty brown eyes out.

Taking a deep breath, I knelt down beside her, gently patting the silky skin of her shoulders.

'There, there,' I said, like a kindly priest at your true believer's deathbed. 'There, there, don't cry, my duck of diamonds. For he is at rest now, and gone to a far better place.'

I sounded very sincere. I almost believed myself. Although a part of me wondered what place could ever be better than the soft bed of Maimiti, the king's daughter.

Sob, sob, sob, she went, the poor thing. The black hair was still covering that beautiful face. I gently tried to pull it away from her eyes, her nose, her mouth – especially that.

'Now, now,' I said. 'Don't cry your little heart out. For old Ned Young is here to comfort you in your hour of need. What can I do to comfort you, my lovely one? Now if we could just slip into these bushes for a moment . . .'

She spat in my face.

A good one, it was – full of feeling and well aimed.

It caught me right on the bridge of my frequently broken nose, and dribbled down that sad excuse for a hooter, the spit only veering off to the right when it reached my upper lip.

Then she was up and screaming at me. Her fists hammering my chest.

And I was too shocked to move.

'You killed Fletcher Christian!' she howled. 'You ugly dog! You toothless old man! You killed my love!'

'I killed no man,' I gasped, and I stepped away from her.

She spat again, this time on the ground.

'You burned the *Bounty*!' she hissed, that black fire in her eyes. 'You killed the only good man among you!'

The funny thing about Maimiti is that she sounded a lot like Fletcher Christian. Because she had learned the lingo from him, I suppose, she had a bit of the dandy and fop in her voice like our poor grilled skipper himself.

But I think that was true of all of us. The ones who learned English, and the ones who learned Tahitian. We all had our language lessons in bed.

She spat a third and final time.

'You remarkable pig!' she growled, and I shivered with shock. For they were the very words that Fletcher Christian had uttered just before we put William Bligh in his boat.

Then she was off down the path and gone, and I knew that she would be watched by other greedy eyes as she tore at her widow's rags.

And I saw that nothing had changed.

We had travelled to the far side of the world. We had suffered storms, inhumanity and thirst. We had been half-drowned, flogged within an inch of our lives and nearly killed because our precious cargo of bloody breadfruit mattered more than our own lives.

We had thrown away England and invited the hangman's rope because we had known true freedom, and all the pleasure of the flesh, and what it means to be loved.

And now we were marooned on the island at

30

the end of the world with no means of ever leaving.

Yet what had really changed?

Nothing.

Our story was still all about the women.

4

The Last of the Rum

Midnight came and the moon rose full and white.

We huddled around a fire on the beach, deciding what was to be done and how we were to live our new lives. We were eight English sailors without a ship.

My jaw was swollen from some awful ache and I chewed bitterly on a short stump of wood. It did no good, but I chewed it anyway.

'Men,' said John Adams with a mighty sigh. 'We are a dwindling band of brothers. There were not many of us when we set sail from Portsmouth and now there are even less.'

Murmurs of agreement around the campfire. I did a quick tally in my noggin, although it wasn't easy with that wretched face ache.

After our noble rebellion against injustice, we had put eighteen men in Bligh's little boat. Thus condemning them, we believed, to certain death in the freezing depths of the Pacific or in the boiling cooking pots of hungry, lip-smacking savages.

Fletcher Christian had set another sixteen men ashore in Tahiti. Some of these were loyalists (there had been too many to fit them all in Bligh's boat). Some were mutineers who were anxious to get back to lovemaking under the palm trees – the fools! Dear old Tahiti was the very first place the King's navy would look for us.

By the time we finally reached Pitcairn there were just nine of the *Bounty* crew left. And now we had lost our captain to an unfortunate fire.

There were the Tahitians, of course. Eleven women, the one with the baby, and a few more already swelling with child, as well as six native men. But I did not count the Tahitians. They did not sit with us around the fire but lurked in the shadows of our new home, jabbering in their own language.

As far as I was concerned, it was just the eight of us left.

Myself.

The godly John Adams.

That drunken scum John Mills.

William McCoy, another hardened drunkard.

Jack Williams – the silent type. Typical armourer's mate. I gave him a wide berth because there was an air of violence about him.

Then there was the four-eyed gardener, William Brown, who liked to call himself a Botanist's Assistant, as though digging up a few breadfruit made him Lord Muck of Cow Shit Farm.

Then there was young Isaac Martin, a good lad who I liked. He was perhaps the only one of us whom life had yet to tarnish.

And finally there was Matthew Quintal, a tall, thin man who sat gibbering to himself as he stared at the dancing flames of the fire. He was mad as a March hare, and marked by God or the Devil for a very sticky end.

But then weren't we all?

'This island is where we live and this island is where we will die,' said John Adams.

I looked at his face through the fire on the beach. I removed the stick from my mouth.

'Unless we are found,' I said. 'Then we will die on the island we left behind, and where our mothers pine for us still.'

Matthew Quintal burbled as though something hilarious had been said.

I glared at him, chewing furiously on my stick.

'Does something trouble you, Ned?' said John Adams. 'I notice you are chewing on a stick.'

'A mere trifle,' I said. 'A slight pain of the jawbone. It is of no matter. Thank you kindly for asking.'

Then John Adams spoke frankly to me.

'Ned, there are some words that need to be spoken,' he said. 'Ned Young, you are rough with your fellow Englishmen and you treat our Tahitian allies even worse, often striking them for no good reason.'

'Thank you, John,' I said.

'It was not a compliment, Ned.'

I looked surprised.

'Truly?' I said. 'Because it sounded like compliment. It sounded like high praise indeed for making an attempt to run a tight ship when others would be happy to whore and booze the day away.' I unfurled my lips at that drunken scum John Mills. 'For someone has to keep order and discipline on this lonely patch of sand we now call home,' I said.

John Adams nodded. 'I agree, we must do better than we are doing if we are to make a success of our new land.' He looked at me. 'But that does not mean a place where men are beaten at will. Ned, it has been brought to my attention that you struck John Mills. And that you have struck other men.'

I was furious at this unjust slander.

'Only Tahitians!' I cried. 'It is true I gave John Mills here my hand for his drunken lip, but I swear the only other men I have struck have been the natives!'

'Perhaps you shouldn't strike anyone,' slurred John Mills, already in his cups.

I was speechless.

'Do you remember what Fletcher Christian said

35

to William Bligh before we left Portsmouth?' asked John Adams.

Jack Williams spoke up. A rare thing for the gunner's mate. 'Mr Christian said, "*There is no glory in it,*"' he growled. 'Meaning our mission. Meaning that there was no glory in men sailing for two years just to bring a cargo of breadfruit to slaves on the sugar plantations of Jamaica.'

'He was very wrong!' cried William Brown, the gardener. 'The breadfruit could feed the slaves of our glorious Empire!'

Matthew Quintal chuckled and leered and rolled his crazed eyes. He was not really joining in the conversation. He was in his own unhinged universe, the great gawky lunatic.

'Fletcher Christian was right!' cried young Isaac Martin, getting all weepy because he missed his old mother's cooking and knew that he would never taste it again. 'Oh, why did we throw away our lives on such a fool's errand? We are lost and damned forever because rich men wanted a cheap way to feed their slaves!'

'But don't you see?' said John Adams, all aglow with the certainty of being right. 'The true glory of our voyage could be here on Pitcairn Island! If we can build a place where men are equal and happy and treated fair and square, then it will be a better place than the England we left behind!'

This went down well.

The drunken fools all started congratulating themselves on their nobility. John Adams' pious goodness was clearly catching. He went on.

'But if we are to make this a happy land, then we cannot treat the Tahitians exactly as Bligh treated us.'

The men were silent for a moment. This clearly did not sound so appealing.

'We must treat all men decently,' said John Adams. 'Brown or white. English sailor or Tahitian native. No man should be master or servant on our fair island.'

'Or we could do it another way,' I said. 'Take one of the natives – any one of them will do, for they are all equally feckless – chop his head off and display it on a sharpened stick as a permanent warning to the rest of the lazy dogs. That should keep them in line without too much wear on the ship's whip.'

Matthew Quintal chuckled with approval. But I was deadly serious. Only a mad man could not see it.

'Hold your tongue now,' John Adams told me. 'No more talk of punishment, Ned Young.'

This riled me. As far as I could see, my captains were all dead men.

'Who elected you master and commander?' I demanded. 'Mr John bloody Adams! The last time I looked, you were an able seaman on the

Bounty! While I was a midshipman! I believe I have rank over you, sir! Mr John bloody Adams!'

'But we are not on the *Bounty* any more,' said John Adams, his eyes now mean slits.

For all his Bible-bashing, I knew he had a temper on him, and I was glad that the fire was between us. I had once seen him shatter a man's jawbone with one punch in a Portsmouth alehouse. So John Adams was not all sweetness, light and gospels, no matter how he played it out now.

'Do me a great service, Ned,' he said. 'Put your stick back in your mouth and keep it there.'

Some of them had a chuckle at that.

But I would not stop.

'And if chopping the head off the first doesn't do the job and put a spring in their step, then take another one of the savages, and then another,' I suggested.

'That's not you talking,' John Adams said, smiling gently now, all forgiving and Christ-like. 'That's just the terrible pain in your tooth.' He nodded with sympathy. 'It hurts you very bad, doesn't it, Ned, my old shipmate?'

'Perhaps just a little bit,' I conceded.

'And it clouds your judgement,' John Adams declared, standing up. He nodded once. 'Hold him down,' he said.

Four of them were suddenly on me.

They held my arms, my legs. There was a knee

on my chest and another on my stomach, knocking the wind out of me. I fought and wiggled and raved and cursed and spat, but they held me down.

'I want that bad tooth out of your head before we talk further,' John Adams told me. 'Let's see if you talk about beheadings when that tooth is out of your head.'

'Master and commander!' I screamed up at him, my eyes wide at the rusty pair of pliers in his hand. 'Damn your blood! Damn your eyes!'

'Give him rum,' commanded John Adams. 'Quickly, now! The rum on his lips, boys!'

We had always used rum for medicinal purposes.

If a man needed his arm or leg sawn off, we got out the ship's rum. If a man needed a tooth removed from his mouth or a native arrow removed from his arse, we turned to the rum.

Only now that pair of drunkards John Mills and William McCoy looked all sheepish.

'The rum is gone,' McCoy bleated.

'Gone?' roared John Adams. 'It can't be gone! There must be rum!'

But of course it could be gone. Because everything that we salvaged from our poor doomed ship would one day be gone. Including our lives. The rum was just the first thing to go.

'Oh well,' said John Adams, bending over me. 'It can't be helped. That bad tooth must come out tonight. Hold him tightly now.'

I could feel the stinking breath of John Mills and William McCoy in my face.

'This is going to hurt you,' laughed Mills, 'a lot more than it hurts us.'

My scream rose to the starry sky.

John Adams, our holy master and commander, was right. Pitcairn Island was a land of plenty. Fruit. Fish. Game. A rich soil and a moderate climate, like a summer's afternoon in England that would go on for all eternity. Everything was there for the picking, the hunting, the fishing, the planting and the taking. Apart from two things.

There was a shortage of women.

And there was a shortage of rum.

Not enough women.

Not enough rum.

And so, to the men who had sailed the *Bounty*, Pitcairn Island would forever be a land of famine and thirst.

They held me down and pulled my tooth out by its blackened root. My cries of agony travelled across the endless expanse of the South Seas, but there was nobody to hear them.

Nobody apart from the Tahitian men and women. They kept well back from our fire on the beach, moving in the shadows, and speaking quietly in their own language.

5

The Woman on the Cliff

I watched the woman as she hunted for eggs.

She was at the top of the white cliffs, peering down at a nest perched on some stumpy branches. I licked my lips at the thought of gull eggs for dinner.

She was some distance from me. I lounged on the beach in a hammock strung between two palm trees, feeling quite exhausted from watching all her hard work.

Even from here I could see the identity of the woman.

Her name was Jenny.

She was my wife.

You might say that Jenny doesn't sound like much of a name for a Tahitian wench. And of course you would be right.

But, you see, some of those Tahitian names were real tongue twisters. The leader of the native men was called Tetahiti – try saying that with your teeth out. Another fellow was Tararu. Then there was Maimiti and Balhadi and Taurua among the women.

It all got a bit much for uneducated seamen like me and my simple-minded shipmates. And that is why some of the Tahitians had proper Christian names that we had handed out with the buckets of glass beads.

So you might see some half-naked devil shinning up a banana tree like a monkey with his tail on fire, and his name might be George. In fact we did have a Tahitian called George, and his climbing was extremely fine.

Or you might see some dusky Tahitian beauty looking for gull eggs on the edge of a cliff, and her name might be Mary or Jane or Jenny.

And so it was.

As I lazed in my hammock, yawning and scratching my arse, the only thing that kept my eyes open was wondering how many gull eggs Jenny would find in that nest.

The gull eggs on our island were large and light blue, speckled with marks of darker blue. We stuffed them into our greedy faces either soft boiled (the white of the egg showing the faintest shade of blue) or fried up in a dollop of fat and served with the day's catch.

Suddenly Jenny straightened, and that woke me up, for I suspected she had spied some fat eggs in the nest. She stood stock still at the top of the cliff, having a think.

The drop of the cliff was quite shallow at the top. It sloped away gently for a bit, like a harmless little hill, covered with these stumpy trees, before it reached the sheer drop to the rocks far below. So as Jenny edged carefully down to the nest, her bare feet seeking grip on the dusty white rock, she must have felt no fear.

I watched her take one scraggy little branch in her hand, and then push her long black hair from her face with the other. She had another think. Then, with her hair shining in the sun, she reached for the eggs in the nest, still holding onto the little branch for safety. Her lovely hair fell forward.

I sat up and smiled to myself.

I could almost taste those gull eggs on the back of my tongue.

But the nest was just out of reach. Those gulls knew where to build, the crafty bastards.

Jenny got on her knees and leaned further out. Then at last they were in her hand. Those light blue gull eggs with their dark freckles. Three of the little beauties, as far as I could see, with one more still in the nest.

Jenny reached for the remaining egg.

I thought to myself, *Soft-boiled or fried in a dollop of fat, Ned?*

43

And then she fell.

The stumpy root that she was holding onto came away all at once. At least, that's how it looked. One moment it was attached to the chalky side of the cliff, and the next it was attached to thin air.

Although the slope of the cliff was gentle, poor Jenny had reached out a long way to steal the eggs of the gull.

And there was no way back.

She fell.

At first she scrambled up the side of the cliff – the top must have seemed so close, and then suddenly so far away.

But she was always falling.

For a terrible second or two she seemed to clutch the gull eggs to her breast, as if she thought that they could still be brought to the dinner table. Then she was sliding down the cliff and the eggs dropped.

And so did she.

She was over the side of the cliff and spinning in the air, always falling, and the rocks were rushing to claim her.

I was on my feet and I called her name.

And I could not stop calling her name.

As if that might bring her back.

As if that might give her life.

Because Jenny was my wife.

And I loved her, you see.

I stumbled back to the camp, my vision blinded by tears.

'Jenny,' I said, my voice all choked with loss. 'Jenny, Jenny.'

I struggled to understand what had happened. I had just watched my wife die while picking eggs. She was on a cliff. Then she fell. It sounded so simple. And yet I struggled to understand how easily happiness could fall apart.

I call her my wife. Of course she was a maid that I met on Tahiti. Perhaps not much of a maid. She had certainly paddled her canoe around the island with the local boys once or twice before I ever dropped my anchor. I do not doubt that.

Still, she was my wife. Perhaps they would not have called her my wife in England, but we were a long way from England. And when she fell, my world fell with her.

I was in the camp before I realised that my shipmates were all stinking drunk. In these early days we still squatted in rough shelters made from palm leaves and bamboo and whatever bits of driftwood we could scavenge from the beach.

Outside these hovels, the sailors loafed about like lords of the realm, rolling with stupid laughter and pawing at any women who were foolish enough to get close.

William McCoy shoved a glass jar in my hand.

'We did it, Ned!' he cried excitedly, too drunk to realise that he was talking to a man with bitter tears on his face. 'We made grog! A good batch of home-made rum! Look!'

Right in the middle of our humble camp, surrounded by the mean grass huts we had assembled, there was some kind of knocked-up device.

It was a big steaming iron pot, pillaged from the mess of our dear departed *Bounty*. A wormy coil of copper connected it to a barrel that had once held our drinking water in the days when we were sailors.

'Take a drink, Ned Young,' McCoy screamed in my face, his reeking breath making me almost puke up my guts. 'It is real grog we have made. Cornmeal, sugar, water, yeast and malt, all mixed up. Then all cooked up. And then we captured the steam in the barrel – and that is the secret.' The drunken oaf took a long glug-glug-glug from the glass jar in his hand and belched like a judge on Christmas day. 'It is stronger than our navy rum!' he yelled.

I looked at their red, sweating faces. There was no sign of the godly John Adams, but the rest of the little crew were all accounted for.

Over William McCoy's shoulder I could see John Mills, my enemy, wiping his mouth on the back of his hand, and eyeing me as if he would like to rip out my throat. Although in fairness, that was his natural expression.

And here was strong, silent Jack Williams, staring into the distance as if he was looking at something ten thousand miles away.

And slightly apart from the rest, Mad Matthew Quintal, babbling to himself and rolling his eyes, like the pride of Bedlam nut house that he was.

Even William Brown, our high-and-mighty gardener, Lord Muck of Cow Shit Farm, had his glasses hanging off of one ear while he absent-mindedly mopped at the vomit on his britches.

Young Isaac Martin was the only one among them who did not look out of his mind.

The gentle-hearted lad sawed absent-mindedly on his old fiddle, a melancholy tune from his Irish homeland, and a glass jar between his legs. The sound of his music stilled my heart for an instant, as it had so often stilled my heart when we were out on the rolling sea. Few things are more beautiful in this life than music heard at sea.

'Take a sip, Ned,' William McCoy urged.

I took a sip.

And spat it out.

McCoy's grog made gnat's piss seem like honey from the bees.

I thrust the glass jar back into his arms and faced my shipmates.

47

'Jenny is dead,' I told them. 'My wife is gone. She fell from the cliff while hunting for my supper and her body was dashed on the rocks.'

Matthew Quintal giggled and rolled his eyes at the news.

I found that I could no longer breathe. My heart felt fit to explode.

'Who will help me recover the poor woman's body and give her a decent burial?' I asked. 'Come on, Matthew Quintal – on your feet. You're not so mad that you can't use a shovel.'

'I refuse!' howled the mad man. 'I refuse and you have no authority to make me!'

'How about my boot up your mad arse?' I said, taking a step towards him. 'Is that authority enough for you, you devil's spawn?'

'What about the natives?' growled Jack Williams. This was a lengthy speech for him, the tight-lipped bastard. 'Get some of those heathens to dig a hole for your dead whore.'

I wanted to kill him. I wanted to throw him from the high white cliffs.

'And stop giving your damn orders,' called my enemy John Mills. 'Did you forget, Ned? There are no more officers and men – only men.'

'On your feet, damn you!' I shouted, unable to stop my bitter tears. 'Help me to bury poor dead Jenny!'

They all had a good chuckle at my broken

heart. Apart from the lad Isaac Martin. The boy looked pained and sawed at his old Irish fiddle, and the sweet music seemed to mourn poor Jenny.

'Will you clap us in irons, Ned?' asked John Mills, leering at me. 'Will you flay our hides with the captain's cat-o'-nine-tails?'

'You mutinous dogs!' I howled, in all my frustration and sickness. 'I might! I might flog you as Bligh flogged you!'

Drunken laughter rolled around our wretched camp.

The botanist briefly stirred. 'But are we not all mutinous dogs?' enquired William Brown, the squint-eyed gardener.

Then he had a modest puke before passing out again.

'Ah, have a drink,' advised William McCoy, so proud of himself for brewing up his barrel of filthy home-made poison. 'We will get you another wife soon enough.'

There was much cackling assent to this suggestion, and then a pair of Tahitian women came into the camp, each bearing a woven basket of still-flapping silver fish.

John Mills and Jack Williams eyed the women and then each other with a terrible hunger.

And they were not thinking about fish.

'But this is tragic news,' said young Isaac

Martin, putting down his fiddle and looking at me with his green Irish eyes. 'Certainly I will help you recover the body of poor dead Jenny, Ned. Let me fetch a pair of shovels.'

'Good lad,' I said, so choked with gratitude to the boy that I could hardly get out the simple words. 'Good lad, Isaac. Thank you.'

And so the youngest among them came with me while the rest of the drunken scum filled their guts with that devil's brew and made life a misery for any woman who got close.

Young Isaac Martin and me buried Jenny close to where she fell, in a sandy cove where you could hear the triumphant cry of the gulls high above. Isaac said a short prayer and we covered her shallow grave with rocks to stop the animals from digging her up.

By the time we returned to camp it was night.

And all hell had been unleashed.

John Adams stood in the middle of the camp, holding out his hands like some great big cross-eyed Jesus of the South Seas.

On one side of the settlement were the drunken sailors. William Brown had supped himself into a state of blackout, but John Mills and William McCoy and Jack Williams and the lunatic Matthew Quintal were all on their feet, brandishing their knives. Their faces were scratched and bleeding, and they roared blue murder at the women on the other side of the camp.

The Tahitian women were also waving knives. Some of them had their clothes torn. All of them were ready to fight or die. There was no sign of the native men. They were keeping well out of it for now.

'Stop this!' cried John Adams, the only thing standing between our camp and slaughter. 'There will be no killing on our island!'

He got that wrong.

6

Crime and Punishment

We watched the horizon.

Where the light blue of the sky met the darker blue of the sea, our eyes strained for sight of a ship.

Every man did it.

You might be fishing for your dinner. You might be picking fruit. You might be laying with your wife under the shade of a palm tree, or blind drunk with your mates on William McCoy's firewater.

It might be the start of the day, or when the sun was setting over Tahiti, the endless ocean and home.

We all tried to fight against it.

But some point in every day your eyes would drift towards the horizon, looking for the black sails of a ship.

You could not help it.

And when a man looked, he could not look away.

I tried to rip my eyes from the horizon. I tried

to order myself not to look. With all the strength in my being, I tried to turn my eyes inwards, to Pitcairn, and our new life.

Yet my eyes would always drift back to the horizon.

I was walking on the cliff where my wife had died hunting for gull eggs, and I came across John Adams, sitting cross-legged with the big black ship's Bible in his lap.

He smiled at me and I sat with him for a while, and he read me a bit from the book. John Adams knew that I did not have the power of understanding the written word.

'*He provides food for those who fear Him,*' smiled John. '*He remembers His covenant forever. He has shown His people the power of His works, giving them the lands of other nations.*' He closed the good book and smiled. 'Is it not true, Ned Young, my old shipmate?'

'It is very true indeed,' I said.

He caught me watching the sea.

'They will never find us,' he said quietly.

I was silent for a moment. But I could not remain silent for long, because I did not believe him.

'They must find us one day,' I said.

John Adams took a breath.

'Pitcairn appears on no map owned by the King's navy,' he said. 'Or when it does appear, it appears in the wrong place. Because of a mapmaker's mistake, Pitcairn is 150 miles from where it is supposed to be. You know this to be true?'

'I do, John.'

'So that is why the navy will never find us.'

'Then they will find us by accident,' I insisted. 'They will find Pitcairn exactly as we found her – by luck. One of the accidents of the sea. They will have already looked for the *Bounty* and they will have already found the men we left on Tahiti. I have no doubt they will have already hung them. They know we are out here somewhere. Now they will be looking for us, and when they find us we will have nowhere to run.'

He could not argue with me.

'Yes, perhaps they will find us one day,' he said. 'But it might not be for a hundred years.'

'Or it might be tomorrow,' I said.

We were both silent for a moment.

'Do you regret burning the ship?' John asked.

'I regret it,' I said, without hesitation. 'Because when we had the *Bounty* we had a fighting chance. If another ship found us, then we could outshoot her or we could outrun her. Now all we can do is swing from the noose.'

His eyes blazed with sudden anger.

John Adams was like a character in the first part of the Bible, and when his blood was up, then fire and brimstone were not far behind.

'Do you know how big this ocean is, you tooth-less oaf?' he roared. 'I tell you that if they ever find this island, we will have long ago died of old age.'

I looked out to sea.

'They will find us,' I said simply. 'And then they will hang us.'

John Adams seized me by the throat. I had not met many men who were stronger than I, but the godly John Adams was one of them.

'If you think that way, then you will go stark raving mad,' he said. 'They will not hang you, Ned. *For you will hang yourself.*'

I could see the truth in his words.

Staring at the horizon, waiting for the ship that would transport us in chains to the hangman's rope, would one day rob a man of his senses.

And in the end it did.

John Adams was right.

But it was not me that went mad.

The grey dawn came.

We were sleeping in our huts when we were woken by a voice screaming from the hill above Bounty Bay.

'A ship! A ship! There's a ship on the horizon, lads! They are coming for us, men! God help us! We are all for the rope!'

We stirred from our beds at this unhappy news.

As we quickly made our way to the hill, every one of us could feel that rope around our necks, choking the life out of us while the assembled crowd leered and jeered and tucked into their luncheon.

The deranged voice belonged to Matthew Quintal, who was always prone to go for a bit of a wander in the night.

My shipmates and I gathered around him while the native women and men chattered in their own lingo, no doubt wondering what was to become of them now that we were for the noose.

'Where, Matthew?' said John Adams breathlessly, grasping Quintal's shoulder in one mighty hand. 'Where is the ship?'

'There! There!' said Quintal, bouncing up and down like a chimp with its bollocks in a twist. 'A ship on the horizon!'

We strained our eyes as they had never been strained before. It was not a clear day and dark clouds hung over the horizon like a small range of ghostly mountains. All we saw was the hundred shades of grey.

'Can you see it?' said William Brown, the four-eyed gardener and the man with the weakest eyes among us.

'I see no ship,' said William McCoy, glowering with fury at Matthew Quintal, his voice thick with last night's firewater. 'I only see a lunatic who we should have pitched overboard for the sharks.'

'It's not a ship,' said young Isaac Martin calmly. 'I think he mistakes a distant cloud for sails.'

'They will put us in chains!' jabbered Matthew Quintal, hopping about. 'They will take us to Jamaica! And we shall dangle! And our mothers shall weep and moan!'

One of the natives laughed.

This set them all off.

Men and women alike.

Soon their brown faces were creased with merriment and their white teeth were showing in the dawn's first light.

For some reason their laughter infuriated John Adams.

'Silence!' he bawled, and they were silent immediately. He took Matthew Quintal in his arms and hugged him like a child. 'There is no ship, Matthew,' he said quietly. 'You are mistaken, my dear old friend.'

Matthew Quintal shook him off.

Then the lunatic whipped out his knife and attempted to slice open the throat of John Adams. It was a wild, slashing blow and missed John's neck, but came close enough to open up the flesh on his cheek. We gathered around John, down on his knees and the blood everywhere, as Matthew Quintal took off down the hill.

'If anyone is going to hang today,' growled Jack Williams, 'then it shall be the madman Matthew Quintal.'

Williams produced his own blade and took off after Pitcairn's resident madcap.

John Mills and William McCoy, both boiling after being roused from their drunken slumbers, also whipped out their knives and went off to hunt Matthew Quintal.

William Brown and Isaac Martin were bending over John, trying to stem the blood that flowed from the wound in his cheek. He pushed them aside to look up at me.

'Ned,' he croaked. 'Are you sure – are you truly sure – that there is no ship?'

I studied the sea, and in that endless blue world, I finally saw what Matthew Quintal had seen.

'There is no ship,' I said, not taking my eyes from the horizon. 'But – my God! I can see a man.'

7

The Shipwrecked Sailor

More dead than alive, the man was flat out on a scrap of wood the size of a coffin.

He floated just beyond Bounty Bay.

At first it seemed that the sea would carry him past Pitcairn. But then the tide seized him, pulling him towards shore. Leaving the native women stemming the blood from John Adams's wound, I raced to the beach with Isaac Martin.

'It's a miracle,' gasped the boy.

'No,' I said. 'Not a miracle. Not unless a ship-wrecked sailor is a miracle.'

The wretch was in the bay but our island seemed reluctant to claim him. Again and again the choppy waves lifted and dropped him. It was a wonder that he was not tossed from his miser-able piece of wood.

As the tide washed him closer to shore we saw that he had lashed his wrists and ankles to his floating grave.

Isaac Martin and I splashed into the water but we could not reach him. There were big rocks at the edge of the bay, and the driftwood snagged against them. The waves pounded the man. I saw his mouth open in shock or pain or prayer.

'The poor wretch is dead,' said Isaac Martin, crossing himself.

'No, he lives,' I said. 'For a while longer at least.'

The driftwood where the man was crucified released itself from the rocks.

It came close enough to shore for Isaac and me to swim out and seize it.

Now we saw the wretch well enough. He was half-starved, half-drowned and roasted alive by the burning sun of many days.

We took our knives and cut the rough twine that had bound him to his raft. Then, as he cried out at the touch of our hands on his poor fried skin, we carried him to the shade of the palm trees.

'You are safe now,' said Isaac Martin. Natives hovered by us, their eyes wide with wonder. 'Bring water!' Isaac told them, and they scampered off to do his bidding.

Maimiti kneeled beside the wretch. She had rags doused in water and she laid them on the man's forehead. The shipwrecked sailor looked up at her lovely face.

'Am I dead?' he said. 'Is this Heaven?'

Then he screamed with pain as the wet rags touched his face, and he knew he still lived in this vale of tears.

Shadows fell across the shipwrecked sailor. The men were back from their hunting expedition. John Adams was with them, a piece of palm pressed against the wound on his face.

'What was your ship?' John Adams asked.

'The King's ship *Patriot*,' the man croaked. 'There was a storm. A terrible storm off the Cook Islands. Lost with all hands.' He began to weep for his shipmates who now fed the fishes. 'On our passage to Tahiti . . .'

We exchanged looks.

Then we were silent, mulling this over.

Was the man from the ship sent to transport us to justice?

'Then you did not reach Tahiti?' I said. The man did not answer. He was off in his dreams. Then Maimiti pressed some water to his parched lips and his eyes flickered open.

'An angel,' he said. 'Oh, Mother – I am in the presence of angels . . .'

Some of the men snickered at that, but I pressed closer to him, demanding my answer.

'You did not reach Tahiti,' I said. 'His Majesty's ship *Patriot* never reached Tahiti.'

'No,' he said. 'Oh – how we longed to see that magical place with all its fair maidens.'

His eyes seemed to swim into focus for the first time.

'But what place is this?' he said. 'Is this Australia?'

More laughter.

My shipmates were a rough and simple crew, who would laugh to see a pudding roll.

'Silence,' John Adams barked. 'This is not Australia, friend. This is Pitcairn. You are among friends on Pitcairn.'

'You are Englishmen,' he said. 'Praise the Lord.'

Then he stopped praising the Lord to cough up some bloody bile.

'He is not long for this world,' said William Brown, as though he were a doctor rather than a jumped-up gardener.

Then Brown's eyes got a steely look behind his spectacles.

'Ask him,' he said. 'Ask him while we still have the chance to ask him anything.'

'What news from England, my friend?' John Adams said.

'And what news of the *Bounty*?' blurted John Mills, that drunken scum.

'And what news of the *Bounty*'s Captain Bligh?' said William McCoy. 'What news of his death?'

John Adams shot them both a fierce look.

But then he turned back to the shipwrecked sailor, for he wanted to know too.

'William Bligh?' says the wretch. 'Bligh is not dead. Bligh lives.'

We were stunned.

'That is not possible,' I said. 'We – I mean, *they*

– put Bligh in a launch just thirty nautical miles from Tofua.'

'And Tofua is teeming with hostile natives,' said William Brown. 'They will put your head on a stick and call it supper.'

'No – William Bligh lives,' insisted the shipwrecked sailor. 'I saw him with my own eyes on the streets of London. And I saw him again on the dock of Portsmouth.' And then he smiled. 'I touched my cap to the great man.'

John Mills whipped out his knife.

'This lying dog!' he said. 'This lying piece of burned meat! I will cut his throat and stop his lies!'

'Put your knife away,' said John Adams, not even looking at the snarling oaf. 'There will be no more cutting today.' He took the wet rag from Maimiti's hands and touched it gently to the shipwrecked sailor's temple. 'Friend,' he said. 'How is it possible for Bligh to live? He was set adrift in hostile waters. And even if he survived the natives on Tofua, he was four thousand miles from civilisation.'

'It's not possible,' I said, looking at the others. 'Is it?'

'William Bligh sailed his little launch four thousand miles,' the shipwrecked sailor told us. 'He sailed it from Tonga to Timor in the Dutch East Indies. He lost a man in Tofua to the natives. He was chased by cannibals in Fiji. He lost five men after landing in Timor. *But he did it.* They are calling it the greatest act of seamanship in the King's navy.'

'William Bligh was a monster,' said Isaac Martin. 'He was a cruel, vicious monster.'

'William Bligh is a hero,' laughed the shipwrecked sailor. 'More than two years after the *Bounty* left England, he reported the mutiny to the Admiralty.'

The men conferred.

It was worse than we could have possibly imagined. Not only had Bligh survived, the fat little devil was considered a hero.

And in our hearts we somehow knew it was true.

When we turned back to the shipwrecked sailor, he was being tended to by the native women. They all loved an English sailor. Especially one on his last legs.

'Mother, I am nursed by angels,' the dying sailor said. 'Is this Paradise?' His eyes swam in and out of focus.

'We are English seamen,' John Adams said, his voice all cold. 'Just like you.'

'But where is your ship?' the shipwrecked sailor asked.

'We have no ship,' I said. 'Just like you.'

He looked at our brown bodies, our tattered rags, our rough features.

'But where are your officers?' he said.

John Mills laughed. 'There are no officers here, mate. Not now Fletcher Christian is gone.'

The man jolted at the name.

'Fletcher Christian? That traitor? That Judas? I have heard that he slipped back into England, cloaked in shame, and that he lives on the streets of London among thieves and whores.'

We all had a black laugh at that.

Already I saw the lies that would be told about us. How the legend and myth of the *Bounty* would be so distant to the truth.

'So that's who you are,' said the man quietly, and he closed his eyes. 'Fletcher Christian's men. Pirates. Traitors. Mutineers.'

'Yes,' I said. 'That's who we are. The men who took the *Bounty*. The men who cast that devil – your hero, William Bligh – adrift.'

'A thousand ships look for you,' he said.

'We took a prison,' John Adams said. 'We took a prison that would have been our graveyard.'

'You took the King's ship,' said the shipwrecked sailor. And then he howled with pain and fear. 'Mother, is that really you?'

'Yes,' said Maimiti. 'I am here, my darling son. Close your eyes. Rest now, my child.'

'Yes, Mother,' he said. 'I know that I will soon be dead. But at least I still have a country.'

He did not say much after that.

The other men wandered off, for there was nothing to see but the last breaths of one more dying sailor. Even John Adams walked away, blood dripping all over his Bible.

But I stayed and watched the native women care for him in his last hour.

He opened his eyes once, to stare at the palm tree where the hunters had hung Matthew Quintal by his neck.

The shipwrecked sailor caught his breath to see the brightly-coloured birds that already picked at the dead man's eyes.

'Is this Heaven or is it Hell?' said the ship-wrecked sailor.

'It is both,' I told him.

8

The Best Time

I bounced the baby on my knee.

'My son,' I said. 'My beautiful boy.'

I lifted the baby high above my head.

He gurgled with delight.

'You are an Englishman,' I told him, and he seemed shocked at this news. 'Yes,' I said, 'you are a little brown Englishman. And one day you will walk down the Mall dressed like a gentleman.'

And at these words my heart was heavy. For I knew that the only way I would return to England would be in chains. But my baby – Captain, was his name – lifted my spirits with his gummy smile.

I smiled back at him, revealing my own tooth-less mouth, so much like his own.

My wife, Jane, looked over from the cooking pot and smiled.

'I must go to the house of Jack Williams,' I said.

Her smile faded and she nodded, for she knew my grim purpose. The wife of Jack Williams, the sister of my own wife, was very ill.

I stepped outside my door with Captain in my arms. The homely sight that greeted us was unrecognisable from the little camp that had been our first home on the island.

Our rough grass shelters were now sturdy wooden cabins. The air was full of the cries of babies and children. Our running – from tyranny, from justice – was over.

We had built lives on Pitcairn.

We had found a home.

Maimiti passed me and I touched my forehead in respect. She nodded coolly. There was a handsome brat squirming in her arms.

She had given birth to Thursday Fletcher Christian a year ago, not long after we buried the shipwrecked sailor. The child had been born around midnight but nobody was quite sure what side of the witching hour. So sometimes he was known as Thursday Fletcher Christian and sometimes as Friday Fletcher Christian. It was very confusing.

With Captain cooing to himself against my chest, we made our way through the camp.

This was the best time – every Englishman had his own wife and cabin now. The native men and the remaining women had shelters down on the beach.

We got on well enough by doing what John Adams told us to do.

There was enough of everything to sustain us. Fish, fruit and women. But the dark times were not far away. Jack Williams' wife had given birth to their baby and it seemed to rip the life from her.

I called Jack's name before entering.

It was dark inside the cabin. When my eyes became used to the light, I saw Jack kneeling over a pale figure on the floor. The new baby cried in its little wooden cot.

'How is she, Jack?' I asked.

He tenderly wiped his wife's face with a wet rag. 'She fades fast,' he said. 'The blood does not stop. Her fate is in the air we breathe. Can't you tell?'

It was true. The cabin smelled of death. A sickly, metallic smell that I was glad to take my son away from.

I stepped back outside and my lungs drank in the sweet pure air. Feeling death breathing on my neck, I climbed to the very top of the white cliffs.

Looking back at the island, and the smoke from the fires in our camp, holding my baby boy in my arms, I felt something that I had not felt for years.

Happiness.

What more could we ask from our home? We had families. We were never hungry. We were never too hot nor too cold. We had stout wooden homes that were better than anything we had ever known in England.

This was the best time.

This was when our dream became real. This was the time when our bellies and our beds were full. The time when we started to believe that they would never find us and that if they ever did it would take them one thousand years.

'Look, Captain,' I said to my son. 'Notice the deeper blue of the sea and the lighter blue of the sky. Do you see, my darling boy?'

Captain showed me his gums and a wave of love flowed through me.

Yes, the best time.

When we all learned to love again.

And then came the war.

9

Civil War

This is how the war began.

When the wife of Jack Williams died shortly after giving birth to their baby, poor Jack was maddened with grief. He roamed the white cliffs with his face twisted in pain, like a wounded animal looking for a place to die.

It was Maimiti who nursed the motherless child. It was Maimiti, the king of Tahiti's proud daughter, who went to Jack Williams' cabin and nursed the new baby as if it was her own child.

And when Jack returned from his mourning, Maimiti did not leave the baby.

Or the cabin.

The first night they stayed together, every man on the island felt a stab of longing. Who did not want Maimiti for their bride? I bet even John Adams dreamed of getting her down on her knees for some good hard praying and perhaps a few hymns.

But she went to Jack Williams. Or perhaps it

was the motherless baby that she went to. But Jack shared her bed.

And what was hard medicine to swallow for the English seamen was pure poison to the native men.

The Tahitian men must have thought that the king's daughter would work her way through the whole of the King's navy before she got around to one of her golden, raggedy-arse countrymen.

They had said nothing when Maimiti lay with dashing Fletcher Christian.

But Jack Williams was just another rough tar with a scarred face and bad tattoos.

And it was too much for them.

The beginning of the war was simple enough.

Jack and I were returning to camp. We had been out fishing and had a good catch of lobster, yellowtail and snapper. A few of the natives were on their way out of camp with their bows and arrows to hunt birds. They stepped to one side to let Jack and I pass. Apart from one of them – a young hothead called Hu.

He had been a boy of fourteen when he went off with Fletcher Christian and the mutineers. Now he was a man of sixteen.

He caught Jack with his broad shoulder and sent him flying.

'I saw that, you filthy heathen!' cried William Brown, the four-eyed gardener.

William McCoy and John Adams were swiftly on the lad, pinning his arms to his side.

'What's to be done with him?' said young Isaac Martin, who I knew to be friendly with the native lad. They were around the same age.

'Teach him a lesson,' said William McCoy. 'School him well, the brown bastard.'

'Aye,' said John Mills. Neither of them were drunk at the minute, but they could not have been angrier in their cups. 'Whip him,' says John Mills. 'Whip him in exactly the way that we were whipped.'

'I'll do it,' said William McCoy, a big grin on his stupid face. 'I'll lay the lash on with relish.'

We all turned to John Adams, who was looking into his big black Bible as if it would have a few suggestions about how to deal with uppity natives. Eventually John Adams nodded his mournful head.

'Hu must be punished,' he said. He looked at the oldest of the natives, an old cove called Tetahiti. He must have been thirty if he was a day. 'I'm sorry, Tetahiti. But I will not see an English seaman struck by a native.'

The *Bounty*'s cat-o'-nine-tails was produced.

We all caught our breath.

The last time we had seen that cruel whip was

out on the open sea, when Bligh was dishing out his rough justice with the biscuits.

I found I could not breathe in the presence of the cat-o'-nine-tails.

We tore off the boy's native garb, his kirtle, and tied him to a tree.

'I am going to enjoy this,' said William McCoy.

As the words left McCoy's leering mouth, Tetahiti came up behind him with a large grey rock.

The old native lifted the rock high above his head and brought it down with as much force as he could muster.

I believe that William McCoy was dead before he hit the ground. Some of his grey brains splashed across my bare feet.

All hell broke loose.

Englishmen and native warriors were immediately locked in hand-to-hand combat.

And then, like a flock of birds acting with one will, the natives broke away from us and headed for the hills of the interior.

We caught our breath and tended our wounds. Then we armed ourselves with knives and went after them.

But the day was almost over now and night falls quickly in that part of the tropics. They were conditions that favoured the game rather than the hunter. We slowed our pace as we entered the green heart of Pitcairn, catching our breath at every strange noise.

The natives ambushed us by the waterfall.

They had been hiding behind the crashing avalanche of water. They came screaming blue murder out of the falls, slashing wildly with their knives.

I saw the death of William Brown, the four-eyed gardener, stabbed in the back by Hu.

And I saw Jack Williams die, his throat slashed ear to ear by Tetahiti – poor Jack dead after just one night of rough love with the King's daughter.

Then we were on them and they were on us.

Men gripping the wrists and the throats of other men. Screaming oaths in terror and fury in the gathering twilight, the waterfall pounding behind us.

And then a single gunshot.

Like the voice of God speaking to Adam in the Garden of Eden.

A long crack that split the air and froze our blood.

We looked at John Adams, the musket still smoking in his hands.

'Enough,' he said. 'No more killing. Not today. Not ever.'

The colour of our skin suddenly mattered no more. Tahitian and English sailor, we walked back to the village, carrying our dead.

The English seamen had lost three men – William McCoy with his brains dashed out as he raised the whip. Jack Williams, the happy groom. And William Brown, the four-eyed gardener, stabbed to death in the ambush. The natives had also lost three of their number. When we gathered once more in the settlement, the cat-o'-nine-tails lying there like the serpent in the good book, John Adams spoke to us in his terrible voice.

'We live together or we die together,' he said. 'From this day forth, we live as equals. Every man has one vote – English seaman or South Sea native, white or brown.'

I snorted with scorn.

'John,' I said. 'Why don't you give a vote to the women? And how about the monkeys? Do the monkeys get a vote?'

John Mills laughed at that, and then his laughter died in his throat. He looked around wildly.

'Where are the women?' he said.

We ran to the cliff top. I had half-expected to see that the women had dashed themselves to death on the rocks below. But no – they were out on Bounty Bay, sailing a raft that they must have been secretly building for months.

'The women grow weary of men,' said Tetahiti, that wise old bird. 'All men.'

The women clung to their raft and their

children. Perhaps they would have made it out to open sea without the babies and the children.

But their squawking offspring howled with terror and clung to their mothers, demanding to be soothed. And one hand for the sea and another for the children was not enough. It was an escape plan that would have required all hands.

The wild waves of Bounty Bay flung the little raft back onto the rocks.

Repeatedly the women tried to escape from our island's water – repeatedly the sea threw them back to Pitcairn.

In the end whatever rough twine had bound the wood of their raft came apart. The logs separated. The raft seemed to melt on the moon-washed sea. The women trod water and held their children above the waves. They believed that they would all now drown.

Down on the narrow sandy beach, we men tore off our native kirtles. We cried out that help was on its way. Then we swam out to the floundering women and children.

And we carried them home to Pitcairn.

10

King of the World

Maimiti smiled at me once.

There had been a time when I had hoped that she might be my wife. It was a mad dream – that the daughter of a king, and the widow of Fletcher Christian, would take the hand of a toothless sailor such as myself.

She was not for me.

But one day, as our children played on the top of the white cliffs, she gave me a smile.

And for those few happy moments, Maimiti made me the King of the South Seas.

Thursday Fletcher Christian was older than my boy Captain. But Thursday – or Friday, as he was sometimes known – was one of those kind children whose joy it is to care for smaller children.

The boys played a game of tag. Captain would stagger on his fat little legs after Thursday. The older boy would let him get just within range and then hop off. They both laughed merrily at this, as did Maimiti and myself.

We sat on the grass as it sloped upwards,

keeping ourselves between the two children and the edge of the cliff. We laughed and laughed at the game our children played.

'They will be great friends,' I said.

'They will be brothers,' Maimiti said, and her laughter subsided to the most beautiful smile that any man has ever seen.

Then she coughed.

Just once.

With her hand over her mouth (she had lovely manners).

And her smile faded when she took her hand away.

I saw the black spot of blood on the palm of her hand.

We gathered the children and walked quickly back to the camp, all laughter gone.

I saw a dead bird on the path, and then another. And then I saw hundreds of dead birds.

Sickness had come to the island.

It was a sickness that came on like a fever.

Sweating. Sore throat. Your muscles feeling as though they were made of lead. But the worst of the sickness was down in your lungs. That was where the sickness began – and where it would seek your end.

My wife was already in her bed, raving with the pain and sweats. Captain bawled to see his mother in such distress. I got wet rags and tried to cool the fire.

Then I picked up Captain and went to see John Adams.

All over the village I could hear the moans and groans of the sick.

'This is a judgement,' John Adams told me, glowering at me from his cabin's doorway like some sun-baked Moses.

'This is no judgement,' I said. 'It is something to do with the birds. Can't you see? They are all dying. And we eat enough of them.'

He had other ideas.

'This island was the Garden of Eden and we were all the serpent,' said John Adams. 'And now comes God's judgement.' The big black ship's Bible was in his hands, but he did not need to read. John Adams knew the words by heart. *'Fallen is Babylon the Great – she has become a home for demons and a haunt for every evil spirit.'*

Captain began to cry a bit at this news.

I picked him up and hugged him.

'John,' I said. 'We must stop eating the birds.'

'A haunt for every unclean and detestable bird,' he continued. *'In one hour she has been brought to ruin!'*

'There is a sickness among the birds on the island,' I said. 'It is the birds who brought it here.'

'No,' said John Adams. 'We carried it with us. From England. From Tahiti. From the *Bounty*.'

A dead bird fell at our feet.

I felt myself growing dizzy. My head was slick with sweat and heat. I staggered where I stood. My small son shivered in my arms. I feared I might drop him and the thought terrified me.

'The sins of the fathers shall be visited on the sons,' John Adams said, his mad eyes rolling.

I cursed him.

Then I saw that he was sick too. That we were all sick.

I walked away, my feet unsteady.

It was as if I was back at sea, and the wild ocean was rolling beneath me.

'Daddy?' said Captain, his face against my chest.

My beautiful boy.

I awoke to a changed world.

My cabin was empty. Outside the island was silent. Not even the sound of the birds disturbed the still air. If I listened carefully, I could hear a soft breeze in the palms and the distant sigh of the sea.

But beyond that, nothing.

It was as if man had stepped on Pitcairn for but a brief moment in time. And now wild nature had returned to reclaim the island.

I left my cabin. I saw no man, no woman, and no child. But as I walked up the little path towards the white cliffs, I heard the voice of John Adams. His words travelled to me through the palms.

'Ashes to ashes,' he said. 'Dust to dust.'

A small white cross stood on the top of the hill.

John held his Bible over a newly dug grave.

Around him I saw only women and children.

I saw my wife. I saw Maimiti. But I did not see young Isaac Martin, that good lad who I liked so well, and I did not see John Mills, that drunken seadog.

I did not see proud young Hu and I did not see the elder, Tetahiti. John Adams walked towards me.

'How long did I sleep?' I said.

'Seven days and seven nights,' he said.

I could scarcely believe it. But I knew that it was true.

'Where are the other men?' I said.

'I buried them days ago,' he said. 'The judgement seems to be on the men. Not the women and children. All of the women have survived. And most of the children.'

And then I understood.

'No,' I said.

John Adams stared at me with eyes that contained all eternity.

'Not my boy?' I said.

John placed a rough hand on my shoulder. 'I am sorry, Ned,' he said. 'It is a harsh judgement that has been passed on our island.'

I could not bear for the women to see my tears. I could not bear to look at that small white cross. And I could not bear to look at the saintly face of the man with the Bible. But I did not run away.

Instead, I took my knife from my kirtle and held it to his throat.

'I thought you wanted to be William Bligh,' I said bitterly. 'But now I see you want to be God.'

He stared calmly at the blade against his throat. Then he smiled.

'You can't kill me,' he said. 'You will have no one to talk to.' His face grew serious. 'I am truly sorry about your son, Ned,' he said. 'I know he was the light of your life.'

I broke down then.

I wanted him to fight me. I wanted him to curse me. I wanted him to tell me that I was damned to the fires of hell.

I could deal with anything but his small act of kindness.

The knife slipped through my fingers. I left it where it fell. And I let John Adams lead me from that heart-breaking grave on the top of the white cliffs and down to the beach.

We sat on the sand and stared out to sea.

I felt myself grow warm although the evening breeze was cool. I felt tired, so tired now, although I had slept for seven days and seven nights. And I knew that very soon I would join my son.

'Rest,' John Adams told me, his voice more gentle than I had ever known. 'Stretch out on the sand and rest your weary body, old friend.'

I felt myself weaken.

I felt that I should lie down to rest for a while – or perhaps until Judgement Day. And so I did. Yet there was no rest. It was becoming difficult to breathe and I was suddenly afraid.

But then my mother was standing by my side, smiling at me, and I felt at peace. Even though my mother died at the other end of the world when I was four years old. Even though my mother was gone at the other end of a lifetime.

But she was smiling at me now, and that was real.

John Adams and I stared out at the bay.

Soon it would be just him and the women and children. It would be a chance to start again. I hoped that he would build a better world than the one we had known.

'Do you remember the night we burned the *Bounty*?' I said.

'She made a grand light,' John Adams said,

and he smiled. 'A light that men will remember for centuries.'

'Good English oak,' I said. 'It makes a mighty fire.'

Departures

Bestselling author Tony Parsons has been appointed
Heathrow's writer-in-residence. The result is
Departures – seven short stories of high drama,
offbeat humour and raw emotion.

Here is Heathrow as it has never been seen before –
a secret city populated by the 75 million travellers
who pass through every year, a place where
journeys and dreams end – and begin.

'A fascinating concept, very well executed . . .
Perfect to dip in and out of.'
Sun

tony parsons
departures

seven stories from heathrow

Quick Reads 📖

Fall in love with reading

Doctor Who
Magic of the Angels

Jacqueline Rayner

BBC Books

'No one from this time
will ever see that girl again . . .'

On a sight-seeing tour of London the Doctor wonders why so many young girls are going missing. When he sees Sammy Star's amazing magic act, he thinks he knows the answer. The Doctor and his friends team up with residents of an old people's home to discover the truth. And together they find themselves face to face with a deadly Weeping Angel.

Whatever you do – don't blink!

A thrilling all-new adventure featuring the Doctor, Amy and Rory, as played by Matt Smith, Karen Gillan and Arthur Darvill in the hit series from BBC Television.

Quick Reads 📖

Fall in love with reading

The Little One

Lynda La Plante

Simon & Schuster

Are you scared of the dark?

Barbara needs a story. A struggling journalist, she tricks her way into the home of former soap star Margaret Reynolds. Desperate for a scoop, she finds instead a terrified woman living alone in a creepy manor house.
A piano plays in the night, footsteps run overhead, doors slam. The nights are full of strange noises. Barbara thinks there may be a child living upstairs, unseen. Little by little, actress Margaret's haunting story is revealed, and Barbara is left with a chilling discovery.

This spooky tale from bestselling author Lynda La Plante will make you want to sleep with the light on.

Quick Reads 📖

Fall in love with reading

Full House

Maeve Binchy

Orion

Sometimes the people you love most
are the hardest to live with.

Dee loves her three children very much, but now they
are all grown up, isn't it time they left home?

But they are very happy at home. It doesn't cost them
anything and surely their parents like having a full
house? Then there is a crisis, and Dee decides things
have to change for the whole family . . . whether they
like it or not.

Quick Reads 📖

Fall in love with reading

Beyond the Bounty

Tony Parsons

Harper

Mutiny and murder in paradise …

The Mutiny on the Bounty is the most famous uprising in naval history. Led by Fletcher Christian, a desperate crew cast sadistic Captain Bligh adrift. They swap cruelty and the lash for easy living in the island heaven of Tahiti. However, paradise turns out to have a darker side …

Mr Christian dies in terrible agony. The Bounty burns. Cursed by murder and treachery, the rebels' dreams turn to nightmares, and all hope of seeing England again is lost forever …

Quick Reads 📖

Fall in love with reading

The Cleverness of Ladies

Alexander McCall Smith

Abacus

There are times when ladies must use
all their wisdom to tackle life's mysteries.

Mma Ramotswe, owner of the No.1 Ladies' Detective Agency, keeps her wits about her as she looks into why the country's star goalkeeper isn't saving goals. Georgina turns her rudeness into a virtue when she opens a successful hotel. Fabrizia shows her bravery when her husband betrays her. And gentle La proves that music really can make a difference.

With his trademark gift for storytelling, international bestselling author Alexander McCall Smith brings us five tales of love, heartbreak, hope and the cleverness of ladies.

Quick Reads 📖

Fall in love with reading

Get the Life you Really Want

James Caan

Penguin

It is possible to get the life you really want.
You just need to change the way you think.

In the thirty years James Caan has spent in business he's learned how to build a very successful company. Using the same business methods, you can build a successful life.

• Discover how to manage your time and money.

• Find out how to set your priorities and communicate well with other people.

• Learn to change how you think so you can use business sense in everyday life.

This ten-point plan will help you achieve your goals, whatever they may be.

Quick Reads 📖

Fall in love with reading

Quantum of Tweed: The Man with the Nissan Micra

Conn Iggulden

Harper

Albert Rossi has many talents. He can spot cheap polyester at a hundred paces. He knows the value of a good pair of brogues. He is in fact the person you would have on speed-dial for any tailoring crisis. These skills are essential to a Gentleman's Outfitter from Eastcote. They are less useful for an international assassin.

When Albert accidentally runs over a pedestrian, he is launched into the murky world of murder-for-hire. Instead of a knock on the door from the police, he receives a mysterious phone call.

His life is about to get a whole lot more interesting . . .

Quick Reads 📖

Fall in love with reading

Amy's Diary

Maureen Lee

Orion

A young woman finds her way
in a world at war.

On 3rd September 1939 Amy Browning started to write
a diary. It was a momentous day: Amy's 18th birthday
and the day her sister gave birth to a baby boy. It was
also the day Great Britain went to war with Germany.

To begin with life for Amy and her family in Opal Street,
Liverpool, went on much the same. Then the bombs
began to fall, and Amy's fears grew. Her brother was
fighting in France, her boyfriend had joined the RAF and
they all now lived in a very dangerous world …

Quick Reads 📖

Books in the Quick Reads series

Amy's Diary	Maureen Lee
Beyond the Bounty	Tony Parsons
Bloody Valentine	James Patterson
Buster Fleabags	Rolf Harris
The Cave	Kate Mosse
Chickenfeed	Minette Walters
Cleanskin	Val McDermid
The Cleverness of Ladies	Alexander McCall Smith
Clouded Vision	Linwood Barclay
A Cool Head	Ian Rankin
The Dare	John Boyne
Doctor Who: Code of the Krillitanes	Justin Richards
Doctor Who: I Am a Dalek	Gareth Roberts
Doctor Who: Made of Steel	Terrance Dicks
Doctor Who: Magic of the Angels	Jacqueline Rayner
Doctor Who: Revenge of the Judoon	Terrance Dicks
Doctor Who: The Sontaran Games	Jacqueline Rayner
A Dream Come True	Maureen Lee
Follow Me	Sheila O'Flanagan
Full House	Maeve Binchy
Get the Life You Really Want	James Caan
Girl on the Platform	Josephine Cox
The Grey Man	Andy McNab
Hell Island	Matthew Reilly

Hello Mum	Bernardine Evaristo
How to Change Your Life in 7 Steps	John Bird
Humble Pie	Gordon Ramsay
Jack and Jill	Lucy Cavendish
Kung Fu Trip	Benjamin Zephaniah
Last Night Another Soldier	Andy McNab
Life's New Hurdles	Colin Jackson
Life's Too Short	Val McDermid, Editor
Lily	Adèle Geras
The Little One	Lynda La Plante
Men at Work	Mike Gayle
Money Magic	Alvin Hall
My Dad's a Policeman	Cathy Glass
One Good Turn	Chris Ryan
The Perfect Holiday	Cathy Kelly
The Perfect Murder	Peter James
Quantum of Tweed: The Man with the Nissan Micra	Conn Iggulden
RaW Voices: True Stories of Hardship	Vanessa Feltz
Reading My Arse!	Ricky Tomlinson
Star Sullivan	Maeve Binchy
Strangers on the 16:02	Priya Basil
The Sun Book of Short Stories	
Survive the Worst and Aim for the Best	Kerry Katona
The 10 Keys to Success	John Bird
Tackling Life	Charlie Oatway
Traitors of the Tower	Alison Weir
Trouble on the Heath	Terry Jones
Twenty Tales of the War Zone	John Simpson
We Won the Lottery	Danny Buckland

Quick Reads 📖

Fall in love with reading

Quick Reads are brilliantly written short new books by bestselling authors and celebrities. Whether you're an avid reader who wants a quick fix or haven't picked up a book since school, sit back, relax and let Quick Reads inspire you.

We would like to thank all our funders:

We would also like to thank all our partners in the Quick Reads project for their help and support:

NIACE • unionlearn • National Book Tokens
The Reading Agency • National Literacy Trust
Welsh Books Council • Welsh Government
The Big Plus Scotland • DELNI • NALA

We want to get the country reading

Quick Reads, World Book Day and World Book Night are initiatives designed to encourage everyone in the UK and Ireland – whatever your age – to read more and discover the joy of books.

Quick Reads launches on **14 February 2012**
Find out how you can get involved at www.**quickreads**.org.uk

World Book Day is on **1 March 2012**
Find out how you can get involved at www.**worldbookday**.com

World Book Night is on **23 April 2012**
Find out how you can get involved at www.**worldbooknight**.org

Other resources

Enjoy this book? Find out about all the others from
www.quickreads.org.uk

Free courses are available for anyone who wants to develop
their skills. You can attend the courses in your local area.
If you'd like to find out more, phone 0800 66 0800.

 Don't get by get on 0800 66 0800

For more information on developing your skills in Scotland
visit www.**thebigplus**.com

Join the Reading Agency's Six Book Challenge at
www.**sixbookchallenge**.org.uk

Publishers Barrington Stoke and New Island
also provide books for new readers.
www.**barringtonstoke**.co.uk • www.**newisland**.ie

The BBC runs an adult basic skills campaign.
See www.**bbc**.co.uk/**skillswise**

Lose yourself
in a good
book with *Galaxy*®

Curled up on the sofa,
Sunday morning in pyjamas,
just before bed,
in the bath or
on the way to work?

**Wherever, whenever,
you can escape
with a good book!**

So go on...
indulge yourself with
a good read and the
smooth taste of
Galaxy® chocolate.